Good-bye, Kitchen

GOOD-BYE, KITCHEN

Story By Mildred Kantrowitz
Pictures By Mercer Mayer

Parents' Magazine Press/New York

For Len

Emily looked at the clock
on the kitchen wall.
It was time, she thought.

She went to the closet and got a small, brown
paper bag. You know, the kind you take your
lunch in.

Then she opened the refrigerator and took out
a bunch of grapes, two apples and one orange.
From the cookie drawer she got two chocolate
cookies—the kind with vanilla cream inside—

and two pretzels, the long ones, all covered
with salt.
She figured she'd need about two hours worth
for the two of them, so she added two lollipops,
one lemon and one orange-coconut, just to be sure.

Then she went next door.

Rufie's mother said she wouldn't be gone long,
maybe two hours or so and, "Rufie, be a good boy.
And here's the key, Emily, just in case..."
Emily said, "Mmmm-m-m," and took Rufie's hand.
They went back to her house because it had a stoop
and they could see better.
They climbed the eight steps and sat down
next to each other.

And they looked up and down the block.
And they played pat-a-cake.
And they ate some grapes from Emily's
watching-food bag, and Rufus said, "Yum-m-m."
So they ate some more. And looked some more,
and waited some more.

Then it came.

It was red. It was big.

It looked at each number on every door
of every house it passed.

Then it honked its horn to announce
its arrival at number 274.

Then the huge doors opened wide,
and a ramp was dropped to the sidewalk.
Bang! Clang!
"Wow!" Rufie liked all the action.

He liked the moving van.
"Brrr-r-r-umba!" he shouted, and Emily
gave him a pretzel, and he waved it back
and forth like a baton, and the show began.

"The kitchen, Rufie. Here comes the kitchen."
Emily closed her eyes.
Oh, how she could remember...

"Good-bye, white dishes with your yellow borders that I had chicken and rice on two nights ago when I was having supper there for the very last time with Junie and Junie's mommy and Junie's daddy and Willy and that silly old bird Margo before they all got into their car and we kissed

and hugged and promised to write every day and
they weren't moving 'so far away that I couldn't
visit, maybe soon, like for Christmas.'

"…and good-bye, flowered tablecloth and white
shiny round table and good-bye, red chairs
with your cold smooth seats and good-bye, forks
and knives and spoons and cake mixer that made
brownies and birthday cakes, and good-bye,
licking them off.

"Good-bye, kitchen!"

Emily opened her eyes.
"Oh, I know what you are, all rolled up
in brown paper and tied with cord! Good-bye
and good riddance, you itchy living-room rug
that I used to sit on to watch television
and tell secrets and play marbles on...
Good-bye, soft green couch with your big feather
cushions that I once slept on all night when
bunk three from Camp Delaware came for a
sleep-over. And good-bye—
RUFIE! WHERE ARE YOU GOING? DON'T LEAVE...
NOT NOW...NOT IN THE MIDDLE OF THE ROOM
I LOVED THE MOST...OH, RUF-F-F..."

But Rufie kept going, down the steps, heading
home.
Emily had to follow.
Rufus was her sixty-five cents an hour sitting job
that was leaving after forty-five minutes.
So she took him to the bathroom, gave him
a glass of water and promised that he could

hold the watching-food bag if he would come
back to the stoop.
Rufus said, "Yum-m-m."
Emily said, "Good boy," and gave him a kiss
and a lemon lollipop.
Rufus said, "Brrr-r-rumba!" and they went back
to watch some more.

Soup, pineapple, paper-towel and applesauce
cartons, all tied up with string, were carried
out of the house and into the moving van,
one at a time.

"Books," said Emily. "I helped pack them."

The last to go into the moving van were the
odds and ends that had been stacked up on the
back porch.
Emily figured they must have moved out the
bedroom furniture while she and Rufie were gone.

Then they closed up the truck.
It grunted and growled and groped its way
down the block and out of sight.
They were gone.

And there was Emily with a funny feeling in
her stomach, a very sad face, two apples,
an orange-coconut lollipop and sixty-five cents
more of Rufie.
I will never find another friend like Junie,
she thought, never in my whole life.
"Follow me, Rufus. Let's go home."
She walked slowly down the steps.

Rufie wasn't following. He just stood there
on the top step, looking down the block.
"Brrr-r-rum-ba, brrr-r-r-um-ba!" he shouted.
This time it was yellow. And it was bigger.
A half-block long, Emily thought.
And it grunted and growled like the one that

had just left, except stronger and louder.
With a huge sigh of relief, it came to a halt at 274!
"Brrr-r-r-um-ba," shouted Rufie. "Brrr-r-r-um-ba!"
Then Emily took two apples from the bag and gave
one to Rufie and they sat down to watch the
second show of the day.

"Why, hello, blue couch. Don't you have lovely,
soft-looking cushions. And I bet I know just
where you're going in the living room, and…
hello, piano! Won't the living room be surprised
to see YOU. And hello, I know what you are,

all rolled up in brown paper and tied with cord
and—RUFIE, LOOK!
"A girl's bicycle...just my size...and look!
A bed, just like mine and—RUFIE, WHERE
ARE YOU GOING NOW?

"OH, RUF-F-F! RIGHT IN THE MIDDLE
OF MEETING A NEW FRIEND!"
But Rufus was finished with watching and the
watching-food bag was empty and Emily figured
his mother would be home by now, anyway.
So she returned Rufus and the key to his mother
who kissed them both—Rufus for being a good
boy and Emily for doing such a good job and,
"Maybe next week about the same time?"
Emily said, "Maybe," and smiled and waved
and left.

Maybe I'll be too busy next week, she thought
as she looked at the big yellow moving van at 274.
She paused outside the house, trying to decide
whether to watch some more. But she figured she'd

had enough good-bying and helloing, and anyway
she did promise to write that letter, and anyway
there would be a lot of helloing tomorrow,
she figured.

So Emily skipped to her door, rang the bell,

waited for the buzz, shouted, "Brrr-r-r-umba!"
and went inside to eat her lunch.

Mildred Kantrowitz is the author of *Maxie* and *I Wonder if Herbie's Home Yet,* both published by Parents' Magazine Press. *Maxie* was selected as one of the Best Books of the Year, 1970, by the *School Library Journal.* Mrs. Kantrowitz studied painting and sculpture at Pratt Institute, the Art Students League, the Brooklyn Museum and the New School. She has worked as an interior display designer and an assistant art director in publishing. Born in Brooklyn, she now lives in the historic Brooklyn Heights district with her husband and two daughters, Amy and Susan.

Mercer Mayer, author and illustrator of many delightful books for children, was born in Arkansas and grew up in Hawaii. He studied at the Honolulu Academy of Arts and at the Art Students League in New York City. He is the illustrator of *Boy, Was I Mad!* by Kathryn Hitte and published by Parents' Magazine Press. Also for Parents' he recently wrote and illustrated *Me and My Flying Machine* in collaboration with his wife, Marianna. Mr. and Mrs. Mayer make their home in the town of Sea Cliff on the North Shore of Long Island.